NIGHT at the FAIR

pictures and words by

Donald Crews

Greenwillow Books New York

*For family,
friends, and
fans — have fun
at the fair.*

For Jack

Watercolors and gouache paints were used for the full-color art. The text type is Akzidenz Grotesk.

*Greenwillow Books, a division of William Morrow & Company, Inc., 1350 Avenue of the Americas, New York, NY 10019.
http://www.williammorrow.com
Printed in Singapore by Tien Wah Press
First Edition
10 9 8 7 6 5 4 3 2*

Library of Congress Cataloging-in-Publication Data

*Crews, Donald.
Night at the fair / by Donald Crews.
p. cm.
Summary: Nighttime is a wonderful time to enjoy the lights, the games, and the rides at the fair.
ISBN 0-688-11483-0 (trade)
ISBN 0-688-11484-9 (lib. bdg.)
[1. Fairs—Fiction. 2. Night—Fiction.]
I. Title. PZ7.C8683Nf 1997
[E]—dc21 96-48780 CIP AC*

MAIN GATE
THIS
WAY IN

PIES
PIZZA
WHALE OH

Nightime
is a great
time to be
at the fair.

Black
skies,
bright lights
sparkling.

FUNNEL CAKES
STEAKS
FRUIT TOPPINGS
LZONE
CORN DOGS
SAUSAGE
Frozen DELIGHT
ICE CREAM
COLD DRINK

So many
things to eat
and drink.
So many
choices.

RACE
-A-
WAY
FUN
RACE FOR
GET
WINNERS
CHOICE
1
2
3
4
5
6

So many
games
to play.

So many prizes.

2 IN WINS
2
IN
WINS
IN BIG PRIZES

And now,
on to the
RIDES!

EXIT

GRAND
CAROUSEL

The best,
the best
ride of all,
is the GIANT
FERRIS
WHEEL!

We get
on at the
bottom, and
when we get to
the top, we'll see
the whole fair.
EVERYTHING!
We'll see where
we've been and
where we can
still go.

WOW!

LOOP-LOOP

THIS
WAY OUT